WORLD'S BIGGEST

Wow.

This is so exciting, Junior! I've been waiting for this trip all month!

I can't wait to see the glow-in-the-dark earthworm! What about you, Laura?

I want to see the Viking replica of Old Bumblyburg! Those Viking helmets are sooo cute.

Whoa! What was that?

I don't know. I've never seen anything like it.

We're next in line!

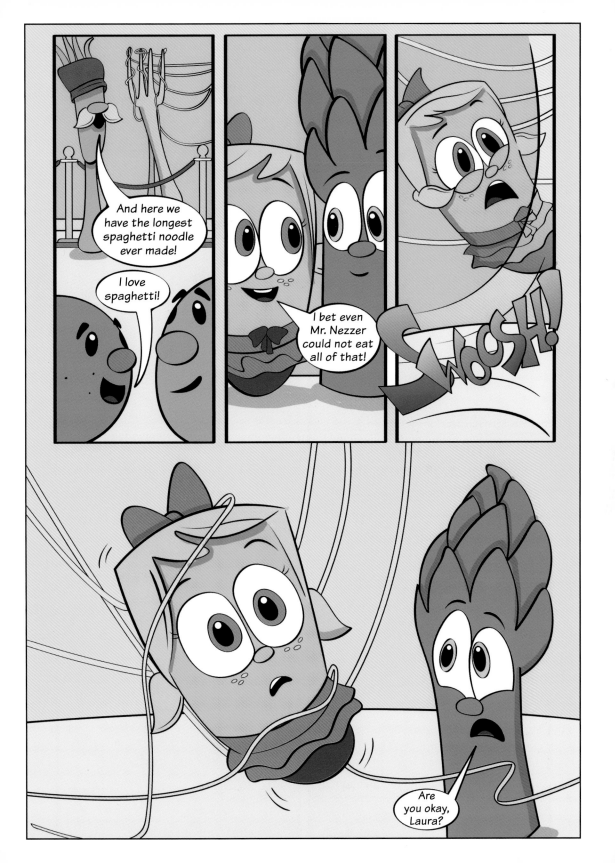

And now, class, we have a very special surprise for you all!

Do we get to see the world's oldest report card?!? I have to know what grades they got!

Even better! If you'll follow the tour guide right into the auditorium on your left, we're about to get a very special presentation from none other than . . .

LarryBoy!

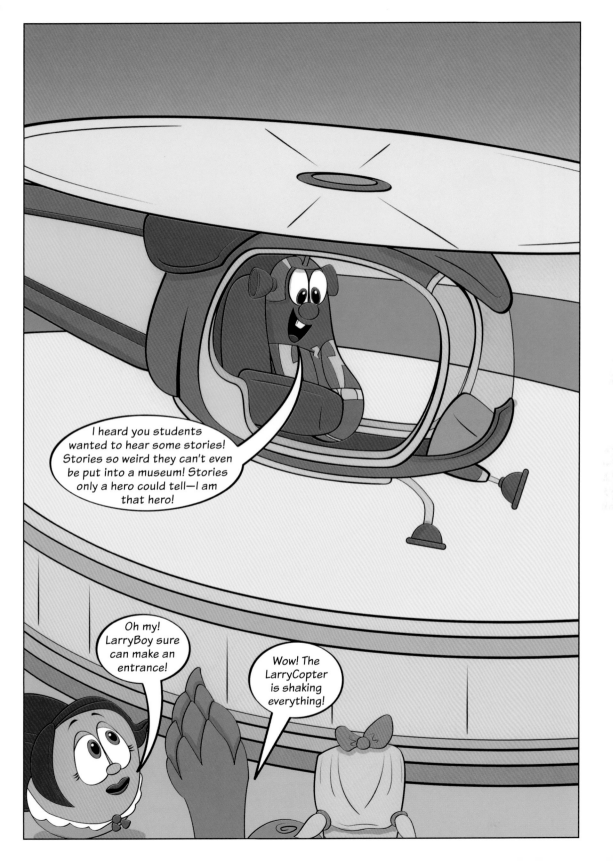

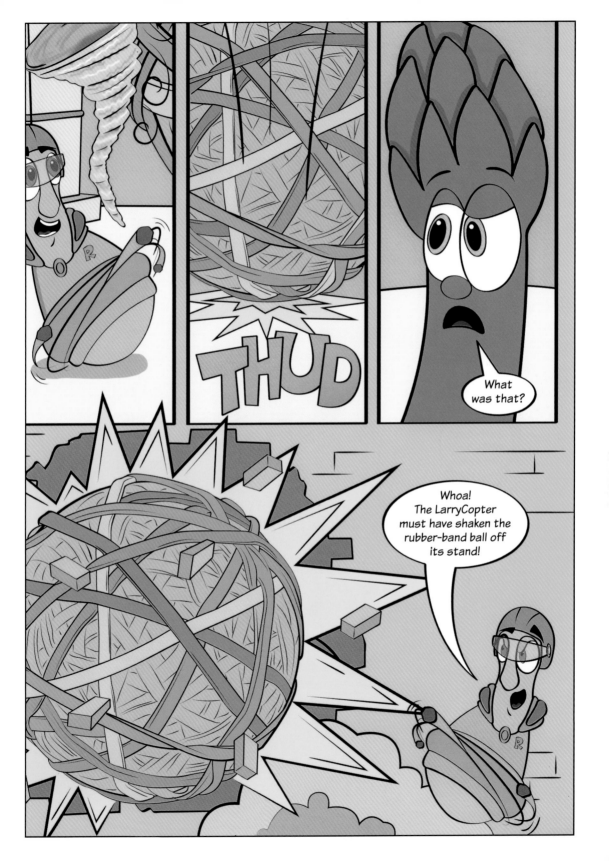

Now, to distract the guards.

No! Come back and close the gate!

And look out below!

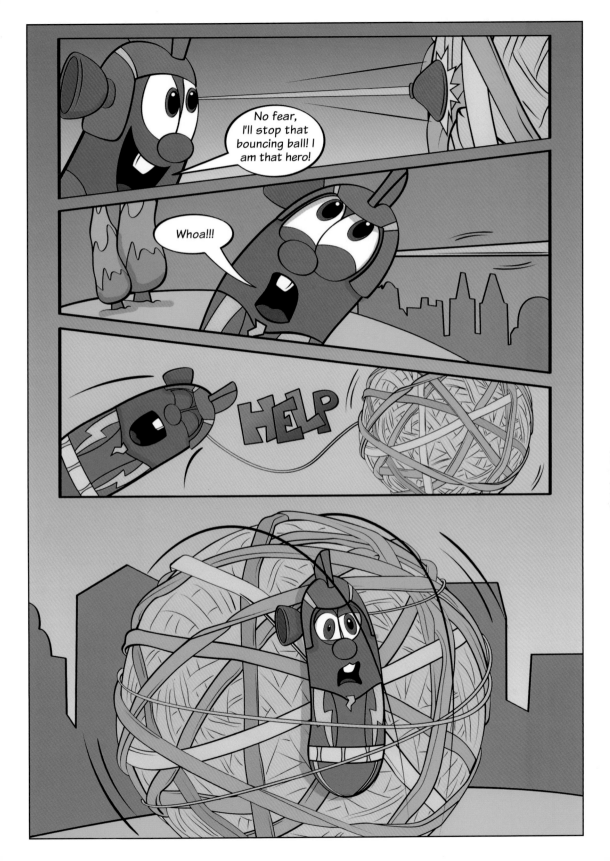

Oh yeah! And LarryBoy! He's your villain now.

You all saw him attached to the rubber-band ball, causing so much ruckus and destruction. Arrest him!

Sorry, LarryBoy. But he's right. We did see you attached to that ball. Why did you have to become a villain?

My kids looked up to you! I even have your action figure!

But I didn't do it! I was trying to save you!

In other news, the mayor is planning to build a statue in the likeness of our new favorite hero, the Ravishing Ruckus.

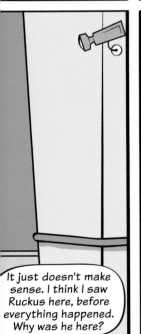

It just doesn't make sense. I think I saw Ruckus here, before everything happened. Why was he here?

Security! Security! I have to look at your surveillance tapes!

For godly grief
produces a repentance
not to be regretted.

—2 Corinthians 7:10 HCSB